E $12.50
Tr   Troia, Lily
           China shelf luxury

DATE DUE

FE 7'9	MY 6'9	
MR21'9	AG11'9	
AP11'9	JUN 14	
AG01'91	OCT 24 96	
DE11'91	NOV 26 96	
JA 3'92	AG 09	
FE18'92	AG 01 02	
AP11'92	OC 22 02	
AP24'92	MY 29 06	
JY16'92	AG 01	
JY30'92	FE 10	
FE 8'93		

DEMCO

CHINA SHELF LUXURY

Story by Lily Troia
Illustrations by Laura Lydecker

Raintree Publishers
Milwaukee

To both my grandmothers,
who have always encouraged me
in my writing. —L.T.

For Charlotte. —L.L.

1 2 3 4 5 6 7 8 9   94 93 92 91 90

Library of Congress Number: 90-41468

Library of Congress Cataloging-in-Publication Data

Troia, Lily.
  China shelf luxury / story by Lily Troia; illustrations by Laura Lydecker.

  Summary: The adventures of a mouse family that inhabits a china cupboard.
  [1. Mice—Fiction.]   I. Lydecker, Laura, ill.   II. Title.
PZ7.T484Ch   1990   [Fic]—dc20   90-41468
ISBN 0-8172-2782-2   CIP
                                                          AC

In the far-off town of Serene Lake lived the Widow Bailey on the old Bailey estate. Although the Widow Bailey and Hannah, her maid, were the only people in the house, there was another family living there. In the fancy parlor, in the china cupboard, lived a family of mice.

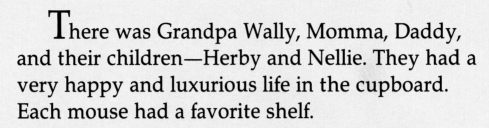

There was Grandpa Wally, Momma, Daddy, and their children—Herby and Nellie. They had a very happy and luxurious life in the cupboard. Each mouse had a favorite shelf.

Grandpa Wally's favorite shelf was the seventh. There, he spent many afternoons dancing with the china doll on top of one of the music boxes. The doll wore a lacy pastel blue dress decorated with dainty pink roses. The doll reminded Grandpa Wally of Grandma Nan, who had passed on several years ago.

Momma's shelf was the sixth. On her favorite shelf, there was an old-fashioned sewing machine. (The Widow Bailey collected many interesting miniatures.) Momma fashioned the family's clothes from scraps of cloth and bits of thread that she found in the sewing room.

Daddy liked the fifth shelf. On that shelf was
a china figure of a man fishing from a boat.
Daddy sat in the boat with the fisherman when
he needed time to think.

Herby enjoyed the third shelf. An army of tin soldiers was set up there. With his sword (a pin taken from the sewing room), Herby pretended that he was a general fighting bravely with his troops.

The Widow Bailey kept her china doll collection and their tea set on the second shelf. Every afternoon at five sharp, Nellie served tea to her doll friends. Sometimes Momma would bring special treats for the tea parties . . . maybe a few crumbs of food or a thimble of milk.

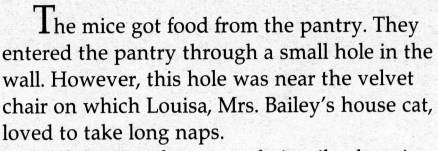

The mice got food from the pantry. They entered the pantry through a small hole in the wall. However, this hole was near the velvet chair on which Louisa, Mrs. Bailey's house cat, loved to take long naps.

With Louisa always on their tails, the mice had many exciting adventures . . . like the time Louisa got locked in the parlor!

The mice usually went to the pantry each day when Louisa was outside taking her afternoon stroll. Hannah always did the cleaning while Louisa was out.

On this particular day, the Widow Bailey volunteered to let Louisa out because she was planning to take a walk herself. Mrs. Bailey, however, was in her golden years, and she forgot.

Hannah began to vacuum outside the parlor door. The vacuum hit the door and shut it tight. Louisa, who was still in the parlor, ran to the door and started to meow. The vacuum was so loud, however, that Hannah couldn't hear a thing.

The mice didn't know what to do. They were hungry and needed food, but Louisa kept pacing nervously around the room!

17

Finally, Louisa fell asleep in the velvet chair. It was still a dangerous trip to the pantry! It was Herby's turn to get the food, but Momma exclaimed, "He can't go! He's just a child."

"I'll go," volunteered Daddy.

"I want to go!" shouted Herby.

"Give the boy a chance. He's got to grow up someday," said Grandpa Wally.

"It's a dangerous job, but he should at least have a try," said Nellie.

"I guess so," Momma agreed. "But you be careful," she said to Herby.

19

Herby climbed down the carved woodwork on the china cupboard. He quietly walked across the floor and through the hole into the pantry. Once in the pantry, he smiled with delight! There on a shelf he saw it—cheesecake! Herby felt like he was in mouse heaven! He climbed up onto the shelf and took a corner of the cake. Then he climbed back down and went over to a crock of pickles. He fished out a pickle, being careful not to fall in.

Herby had his hands full. He wondered how he was going to carry the food back. Then he noticed a lonesome tea bag on the floor. He could drag the food on top of the tea bag! The adults would enjoy a cup of tea. Tea was bitter without sugar, so Herby climbed back up to the shelf to get a sugar cube from the bowl.

Herby loaded the food onto the tea bag and dragged it all to the hole in the wall. Luckily, Louisa was still sleeping. But, as Herby pulled the food into the parlor, the sugar cube fell off. It rolled noisily across the floor and hit the chair leg.

Herby froze solid with fright! Louisa woke up, and jumped off the chair. Herby made a mad dash for the curtains, leaving the food behind. He scrambled up the curtains, clinging to them for dear life.

Louisa batted the curtains and meowed furiously. There was only one way for Herby to get to the china cupboard safely. When the curtains swung toward the cupboard, Herby jumped into the air with all his might. He grabbed onto the handle of the cupboard and climbed in.

Just then the parlor door opened. The mice quickly hid as Hannah walked in. She exclaimed, "There you are, Louisa! Mrs. Bailey and I have been worried about you."

Hannah took Louisa out. Luckily, she didn't see the food under the chair.

Herby, Nellie, and Daddy climbed down and brought the food up together.

All the mice sat down to a joyous meal of tea (with sugar), pickle, and cheesecake. Herby felt proud that he had provided his family with such delicious food. That night the mouse family gave thanks that they were all together, safe and sound.

Lily Troia wrote her first book at the age of four. She published it herself, using two pieces of cardboard!

Lily wrote the whimsical **China Shelf Luxury** when she was in the fourth grade. She was inspired to write about a tiny world inhabited by mice because she is fascinated with the idea of miniatures.

Lily attends Park Falls Elementary School in Park Falls, Wisconsin, where she is an excellent student. Her favorite subjects are math and music. She also enjoys reading, sewing, swimming, and playing the piano. She is active in Girl Scouts.

Although Lily lives in rural Wisconsin, she loves traveling to the big city of Chicago to visit her grandparents and cousins and to spend time in the museums. She has a younger sister, Donna Ellen, and a black cocker spaniel named Buster.

It has always been a dream of Lily's to be a published author. Besides writing stories, Lily also writes poetry. When Lily grows up, she wants to be a physicist, a writer, or a lawyer. Lily's parents are Catherine and Nathan Troia.

The twenty honorable-mention winners in the **1990 Raintree Publish-A-Book Contest** were: Della Armstrong of Moyie Springs, Idaho; Alane Benson of McKeesport, Pennsylvania; Jonathan Caton of Flossmoor, Illinois; Gabriel Chrisman of Bainbridge Island, Washington; Christy Druml of Waukesha, Wisconsin; Rebecca L. Emmel of Sandpoint, Idaho; Nicole Estvanik of Enfield, Connecticut; Amanda M. Frank of Slinger, Wisconsin; Lara Garraghty of Goode, Virginia; Andrea Jauregui of Syosset, New York; Aynsley Kenner of Mesa, Arizona; Dharma C. Lawrence of Spring, Texas; Jackie Lyn Leavitt of Idaho Falls, Idaho; Darren Ruthenbeck of Carmichael, California; Tim Schlosser of Durand, Wisconsin; Blake Smisson of Fort Valley, Georgia; Tori Smith of Walkerton, Indiana; Pia Suparak of San Dimas, California; Christy Williams of Mt. Dora, Florida; and Stephanie York of Edmonton, Kentucky.

Artist Laura Lydecker, who lives in Maryland, attended Parsons School of Design in New York City. She has been illustrating for the past fifteen years. She and her husband, Jeff Carr, a painter, have a daughter named Charlotte. Whenever Laura has a free moment between illustration, housework, errands, and being a busy mother, she loves to garden.